The Story of
SHERLOCK HOLMES
the Famous Detective

Sherlock Holmes and his helpful friend Dr. John Watson are fictional characters created by British writer Sir Arthur Conan Doyle. Doyle published his first novel about the pair, *A Study in Scarlet,* in 1887, and it became very successful. Doyle went on to write fifty-six short stories, as well as three more novels about Holmes's adventures—*The Sign of Four* (1890), *The Hound of the Baskervilles* (1902), and *The Valley of Fear* (1915).

Sherlock Holmes and Dr. Watson have become some of the most famous book characters of all time. Holmes spent most of his time solving mysteries, but he also had a wide array of hobbies, such as playing the violin, boxing, and sword fighting. Watson, a retired army doctor, met Holmes through a mutual friend when Holmes was looking for a roommate. Watson lived with Holmes for several years at 221B Baker Street before marrying and moving out. However, after his marriage, Watson continued to assist Holmes with his cases.

The original versions of the Sherlock Holmes stories are still printed, and many have been made into movies and television shows. Readers continue to be impressed by Holmes's detective methods of observation and scientific reason.

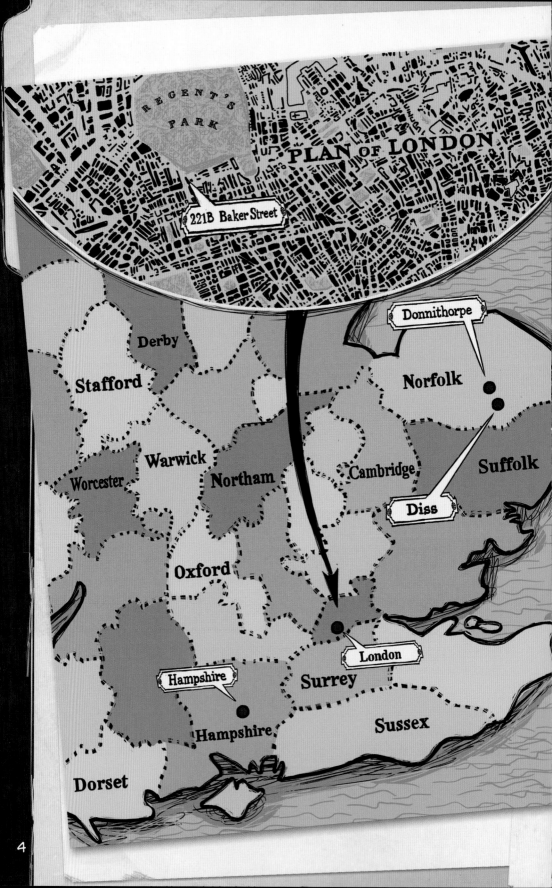

SHERLOCK HOLMES

and the *Gloria Scott*

Based on the stories of
Sir Arthur Conan Doyle

Adapted by **Murray Shaw** and **M. J. Cosson**
Illustrated by **Sophie Rohrbach** and **JT Morrow**

GRAPHIC UNIVERSE™ · MINNEAPOLIS · NEW YORK

Grateful acknowledgment to Dame Jean Conan Doyle for permission to use the Sherlock Holmes characters created by Sir Arthur Conan Doyle

Graphic Universe™
A division of Lerner Publishing Group, Inc.
241 First Avenue North
Minneapolis, MN 55401 U.S.A.

Website address: www.lernerbooks.com

Library of Congress Cataloging-in-Publication Data

Shaw, Murray.
    Sherlock Holmes and the Gloria Scott / based on the stories of Sir Arthur Conan Doyle ; adapted by Murray Shaw and M.J. Cosson ; illustrated by Sophie Rohrbach and JT Morrow.
        p.   cm. — (On the case with Holmes and Watson ; #14)
    Summary: Retold in graphic novel form, Sherlock Holmes investigates a mystery involving the father of an old friend, who seems to be under the threat of blackmail. Includes a section explaining Holmes's reasoning and the clues he used to solve the mystery.
    ISBN: 978-0-7613-7093-2 (lib. bdg. : alk. paper)
    1. Graphic novels. (1. Graphic novels. 2. Doyle, Arthur Conan, Sir, 1859-1930. Adventure of the Gloria Scott—Adaptations. 3. Mystery and detective stories.) I. Cosson, M. J. II. Rohrbach, Sophie, ill. III. Morrow, J. T., ill. IV. Doyle, Arthur Conan, Sir, 1859-1930. Adventure of the Gloria Scott. V. Title.
    PZ7.7.S46Sie 2012
    741.5'973—dc23   2011021820

Manufactured in the United States of America
1 – DP – 12/31/11

Young Sherlock Holmes

Sherlock Holmes   Dr. Watson

Victor Trevor   Justice Trevor

Hudson

Evans

Maid   Butler

Wilson

Tom Prendergast

5

From the Desk of
John H. Watson, M.D.

My name is Dr. John H. Watson. For several years, I have been assisting my friend, Sherlock Holmes, in solving mysteries throughout the bustling city of London and beyond. Holmes is a peculiar man—always questioning and reasoning his way through various problems. But when I first met him in 1878, I was immediately intrigued by his oddities.

Holmes has always been more daring than I, and his logical deduction never ceases to amaze me. I have begun writing down all of the adventures I have with Holmes. This is one of those stories.

Sincerely,

Dr. Watson

7

This excited my curiosity. I had tried many times to get Holmes to tell me how he had become interested in the detection of crime. In fact, I had nearly given up asking and had become used to his silence on the subject.

Holmes explained that the Trevor estate was near Diss in the county of Norfolk. It had an old manor house with solid oak beams and brick walls. The woods provided excellent hunting of pheasant and wild duck, and there was good fishing in the stream.

17

Holmes explained that having regained his calm, the justice sat back to enjoy his cheese and bread pudding. But every so often during Holmes's stay, he would catch the man looking closely at him, as if measuring his intentions.

Then, one afternoon, while on the garden lawn, a maid arrived with an announcement. A certain Mr. Hudson had come calling to see Justice Trevor.

Holmes explained that in the days that followed, nothing seemed to satisfy Hudson. He was made gardener and then butler's assistant. But still he complained. He ordered the other servants about as if he owned the place.

Finally, Victor could stand it no longer. He threw Hudson out of the house. But Hudson immediately went to Justice Trevor demanding an apology.

MY BOY, PERHAPS YOU'VE BEEN A LITTLE TOO HARD ON MR. HUDSON.

I'VE NOT BEEN HARD ENOUGH, AND NEITHER HAVE YOU. THIS MAN IS THE VERY DEVIL. WE HAVE NOT HAD A PEACEFUL HOUR SINCE HIS ARRIVAL.

I KNOW WHEN I'M NOT WANTED. I'LL GO TO BEDDOES IN HAMPSHIRE THEN.

LATER, WE FOUND MR. TREVOR IN THE STUDY, DRUNK ONCE MORE. HE APOLOGIZED FOR THE STATE WE FOUND HIM IN.

VICTOR, YOU'LL NOT THINK POORLY OF YOUR FATHER, NOW WILL YOU?

NO, SIR.

LESS THAN A WEEK LATER, I RECEIVED A TELEGRAM FROM VICTOR, ASKING ME TO COME BACK TO DONNITHORPE IMMEDIATELY. HE MET ME AT THE DISS STATION.

SHERLOCK, MY FATHER IS DYING.

IS IT HIS HEART?

NO, IT'S A KIND OF STROKE. THE DOCTOR FEARS HE SHALL NOT COME OUT OF IT.

WHAT BROUGHT IT ON?

IT'S SO STRANGE. THIS LETTER ARRIVED BY POST FROM HAMPSHIRE. MY FATHER READ IT AND BEGAN SHAKING UNCONTROLLABLY. THEN HE FELL DOWN, UNCONSCIOUS.

The supply of game for London is going steadily up. Head-keeper Hudson, we believe, has now been told to receive all orders for fly-paper and for preservation of your hen-pheasant's life.

25

At this point, Holmes had his first look at this unusual message. As they traveled back to the estate, he tried to find the meaning hidden in it. Since it was posted in Hampshire and mentioned Hudson, the note was obviously from Beddoes.

Holmes tried reading the note backward. But it made no sense. Reading every other word shed no light on the meaning either. Then, in an instant, he could see it. The solution was to read every third word:

THE supply of *GAME* for London *IS* going steadily *UP*. Head-Keeper *HUDSON,* we believe, *HAS* now been *TOLD* to receive *ALL* orders for *FLY*-paper and *FOR* preservation of *YOUR* hen-pheasant's *LIFE*.

So the real message was: The game is up. Hudson has told all. Fly for your life.

OF COURSE.

IT WAS IN THESE PAPERS THAT WE DISCOVERED THE FULL STORY OF JUSTICE TREVOR'S PAST AND WHY HE WAS SO EASY ON HUDSON.

AT THE TIME, MY NAME WAS JACK ARMITAGE, NOT TREVOR.

IN THE CELL TO MY RIGHT WAS EVANS, A YOUNG MAN WHO HAD COMMITTED A CRIME LIKE MINE. AND IN THE CELL TO MY LEFT WAS TOM PRENDERGAST. HE HAD BEEN PUT IN PRISON BECAUSE HE HAD STOLEN VAST AMOUNTS OF MONEY FROM LONDON MERCHANTS.

PRENDERGAST HAD PLANS.

LISTEN, ARMITAGE. I HAVE A FRIEND ON BOARD—WILSON, THE CHAPLAIN. HE'S NOT A REAL CHAPLAIN.

HE'S NOT?

NO SIREE. HE'S COME ABOARD WITH MY MONEY. HE'S GOING TO TAKE CARE OF US RIGHT SMART. HE'S BOUGHT OFF MOST OF THE CREW AND THE SOLDIERS. IN TWO DAYS, WE'RE TAKING OVER THIS SHIP.

ARE YOU AND YOUR FRIEND EVANS WITH US ON THIS?

THE PRISONER WRESTLED THE GUN AWAY FROM THE DOCTOR.

THEN THE PRISONER TIED HIM UP.

THE PRISONER HELD THE GUN ON THE DOCTOR AND SOUNDED THE SIGNAL FOR THE REVOLT.

Tweet-tweet-tweet-tweet!

FINALLY, THE SHIP *HOTSPUR* SPOTTED US.

AHOY!

BUT BEFORE WE WENT ABOARD, WE ALL VOWED NOT TO TELL THE FATE OF THE *GLORIA SCOTT*. I ONLY TELL YOU NOW, MY SON, SO YOU CAN UNDERSTAND WHY I FEAR DISGRACE.

The *Gloria Scott*: How Did Holmes Solve It?

How did Holmes deduce that the tattoo was involved in Justice Trevor's secret?

Holmes noticed the initials J.A. tattooed on Trevor's arm. When Holmes mentioned them, Trevor fainted and then acted suspiciously. Trevor made the excuse that the initials were those of a woman he had once loved. Holmes was not totally satisfied. Later, when Holmes read the justice's papers, he discovered that J.A. stood for Trevor's real name—Jack Armitage.

How did Holmes figure out that the sea voyage had a bearing on Justice Trevor's fear?

When Hudson arrived and Justice Trevor mentioned that he and Hudson had been shipmates, Holmes began to watch the two of them for clues. Trevor started to drink and act strangely immediately after Hudson's arrival. Holmes suspected that Hudson had some kind of power over Trevor. Holmes then wondered if something unusual had happened on the sea voyage they had once shared.

How did Holmes break the code of the strange message?

When Holmes read the oddly worded message, he was drawn to the unusual spelling of the words head-keeper and fly-paper. Since both words are usually written without hyphens, Holmes figured the hyphens were the key to the hidden message. He made the terms into separate words: game, keeper, fly and paper. Then he tried to read the message using different word combinations. He found that reading every third word made an understandable message.

How did Holmes know that the message contained a code and that the message related to Trevor's problem?

Holmes figured that Beddoes and Trevor had agreed upon this three-word code long ago. Trevor had probably received a coded message from Beddoes earlier that year warning him about Hudson's arrival in England. That was why Trevor had had the head of his cane filled with lead.

Further Reading and Websites

Boissery, Beverley. *Sophie's Exile*. New York: Boardwalk Books, 2008.

Clarke, Mary Higgins. *Ghost Ship*. New York: Simon & Schuster Children's Books, 2007.

Convicts to Australia
http://members.iinet.net.au/~perthdps/convicts

Costain, Meredith. *You Wouldn't Want to Be an 18th-Century British Convict!: A Trip to Australia You'd Rather Not Take*. Danbury, CT: Children's Press, 2007.

O'Brian, Patrick. *The Mutiny on the Bounty*. New York: Walker & Company, 2007.

Peacock, Shane. *Eye of the Crow: The Boy Sherlock Holmes*. Toronto: Tundra, 2009.

Sherlock Holmes Museum
http://www.sherlock-holmes.co.uk

221 Baker Street
http://221bakerstreet.org

About the Author

Sir Arthur Conan Doyle was born on May 22, 1859. He became a doctor in 1882. When this career did not prove successful, Doyle started writing stories. In addition to the popular Sherlock Holmes short stories and novels, Doyle also wrote historical novels, romances, and plays.

About the Adapters

Murray Shaw's lifelong passion for Sherlock Holmes began when he was a child. He was the author of the Match Wits with Sherlock Holmes series published in the 1990s. For decades, he was a popular speaker in public schools and libraries on the adventures of Holmes and Watson.

M. J. Cosson is the author of more than fifty books, both fiction and nonfiction, for children and young adults. She has long been a fan of mysteries and especially of the great detective, Sherlock Holmes. In fact, she has participated in the production of several Sherlock Holmes plays. A native of Iowa, Cosson lives in the Texas Hill Country with her husband, dogs, and cat.

About the Illustrators

French artist Sophie Rohrbach began her career after graduating in display design at the Chambre des Commerce. She went on to design displays in many top department stores including Galerias Lafayette. She also studied illustration at Emile Cohl school in Lyon, France, where she now lives with her daughter. Rohrbach has illustrated many children's books. She is passionate about the colors and patterns that she uses in her illustrations.

JT Morrow has worked as a freelance illustrator for over twenty years and has won several awards. He specializes in doing parodies and imitations of the Old and Modern Masters—everyone from da Vinci to Picasso. JT also exhibits his paintings at galleries near his home. He lives just south of San Francisco with his wife and daughter.